Fairy Dust

D1385676

Book Four

Fairy Dust

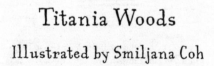

Titania Woods

Illustrated by Smiljana Coh

BLOOMSBURY

LONDON BERLIN NEW YORK

To my husband

Bloomsbury Publishing, London, Berlin and New York

First published in Great Britain in 2008 by Bloomsbury Publishing Plc
36 Soho Square, London, W1D 3QY

This edition published in 2009

Text copyright © Lee Weatherly 2008
Illustrations copyright © Smiljana Coh 2008
The moral rights of the author and illustrator have been asserted

A CIP catalogue record of this book is available from the British Library

ISBN 978 1 4088 0489 6

FSC
Mixed Sources
Product group from well-managed
forests and other controlled sources
Cert no. SGS - COC - 2061
www.fsc.org
© 1996 Forest Stewardship Council

Typeset by Dorchester Typesetting Group Ltd
Printed in Great Britain by Clays Ltd, St Ives Plc

1 3 5 7 9 10 8 6 4 2

www.glitterwingsacademy.co.uk

Chapter
One

'Isn't it great to be going back to Glitterwings?' said Twink Flutterby to her best friend, Bimi Bluebell. 'I can hardly wait to see everyone again!' Twink's lavender wings blurred as she did a quick somersault in the air.

Bimi smiled in agreement as the two fairies flew through the misty winter morning. 'We had a fabulous holiday, though, didn't we? I can't believe it's over already.'

Twink nodded, eyes shining. 'It was completely glimmery! You'll have to come to stay with us again this summer.'

Bimi had stayed with the Flutterby family for the last week of the winter holidays, and the two friends had had a wonderful time. Twink's family lived beside a stream in a grassy meadow, and she and Bimi had gone skating on the frozen water with Teena, Twink's younger sister – first flying overhead to get their speed up, and then touching down and shooting across the ice like rockets, screaming with laughter. Brownie, the Flutterbys' mouse, had cavorted with them, skidding and sliding across the frozen surface.

Then for the last few days, they had stayed with Twink's grandmother in her cosy woodland stump. The kind old fairy had thoroughly spoiled the girls with freshly baked honey cakes, and let them stay up late to hear stories about when she was a young fairy.

Twink banked to avoid an icy cobweb, and sighed happily. It had been such a brilliant holiday, but she'd be glad to get back to Glitterwings Academy. The giant oak tree felt like home now.

'And just think!' added Bimi. 'Next term we'll be Second Years!'

Excitement shivered across Twink's wings. 'Won't that be fantastic? We'll be able to use fairy dust then, and all sorts!'

Twink's father, flying a little way ahead of them, laughed. 'I shudder to think what you girls will get up to with fairy dust,' he teased over his shoulder. 'Better just stay First Years; it's a lot safer for everyone.'

Twink made a face at her father, and then she and Bimi burst into laughter. 'Oh, dear – imagine Sooze using fairy dust!' giggled Bimi.

'Yes, maybe Dad's right,' said Twink with a grin. She and Sooze had once been best friends, and she knew all too well how impulsive the lavender-haired fairy could be. At least she had the best friend in the world in Bimi now!

Twink glanced across at her, struck anew by how pretty Bimi was. She had gleaming dark-blue hair, and silver wings with an unusual swirling pattern of gold. When Twink had first met Bimi, she had thought she was stuck-up. But Bimi was actually very shy, and hated attention being drawn to her looks.

'Girls, we're almost there,' called Twink's mother. 'Look, Glitterwings is coming into view.'

Twink and Bimi exchanged an eager glance. Putting on a burst of speed, they jetted over the frozen grass, up a small hill – and then stopped with a cry of delight.

'It's beautiful!' breathed Twink.

Twink's mother smiled as she flew up beside them. 'It's always beautiful in winter term,' she said. 'I used to think it was my –'

'Favourite term of all!' finished Twink's father with a mischievous grin.

Twink and Bimi laughed as her mother pretended to swat her dad's arm. Maybe Twink's mother said the same thing every term, but their school did look extremely pretty! The great oak tree that housed Glitterwings Academy sparkled in the grey mist, its bare branches white with frost. Hundreds of tiny golden windows wound their way up its trunk, and the grand double doors at its base seemed to smile in welcome.

'But – where is everyone?' said Bimi. 'It looks abandoned!'

Twink frowned. Bimi was right. On the first day of a new term there were usually crowds of young fairies hovering outside the tree, chattering and laughing as they shared their holiday adventures. But now there was no one in sight.

'Maybe it's too cold for everyone,' said Twink's mother. 'They're all inside, warming their wings!'

'Maybe,' said Twink doubtfully.

Suddenly Bimi gave a gasp. 'Look at the pond!'

Twink spun about in the air. Her eyes widened. The school's pond lay a little way away, its surface hard and frozen. And rising up from its centre was a tall, shining pole made of ice. Hundreds of frosty strands flowed down from its top, like icy hair.

Suddenly the mystery of the abandoned school was solved. Everyone was down at the pond. The school's fairies hovered above the bank in brightly coloured clusters, buzzing excitedly.

'What *is* it?' wondered Bimi.

'An ice pole!' murmured Twink's father.

Twink and Bimi looked at each other, puzzled. 'What's an ice pole?' asked Twink.

But her parents had fallen unusually quiet. Twink's father put his arm around her mother. They hovered side by side, gazing down at the ice pole with faraway smiles on their faces.

Twink stared at them, and then glanced at Bimi. Her best friend looked as confused as she felt.

'Oh, it's a lovely one,' sighed Twink's mother. 'I wish we could be here to see it!'

'See what?' asked Twink.

But her father just shook himself and grinned. 'Well, Twinkster, I think you're going to have a very interesting term!'

'But what –' started Twink.

'Write often, darling.' Twink's mother gave her and Bimi quick hugs, rubbing her wings against theirs. 'And we're so proud of both of you already! It's a great honour, you know.'

'*What's* a great honour?' cried Twink, half-laughing in exasperation.

Her father chuckled and handed them their oak-leaf bags. 'Better let Miss Shimmery tell you. Have a good term, girls. You'll always remember it, that's for sure!'

As Twink's parents flew away, Twink and Bimi looked at each other. 'What was *that* all about?' said Bimi. 'It's not like your parents to be so mysterious!'

Twink shrugged in bewilderment. 'Come on – let's get a closer look!'

The cold wind whistled through their wings as the two girls zoomed down to the pond. They flitted in and out of the crowd of chattering fairies, trying to get a closer look at the ice pole.

'Look, there's Pix!' said Twink, spying another fairy from Daffodil Branch. The clever red-headed fairy was hovering with a few others from their branch. As Twink and Bimi joined them there were squeals of welcome, and quick hugs and flutters.

'But what *is* that thing?' asked Twink finally, gazing at the pole. 'My parents called it an ice pole, but they wouldn't tell us what it's for!'

Pix shook her head. 'Nobody knows. It just appeared over the holidays.'

Up close, the ice pole was even more impressive. Detailed ice-carvings of every creature imaginable glistened from its surface. The long, frozen strands that flowed from its top made a noise like little bells as they clinked against each other in the breeze. The whole world seemed to go still as Twink stared at it. It was so mysterious, and so beautiful!

'Is it magic?' she heard someone whisper.

'Definitely,' replied one of the older girls. 'And not fairy magic, either.'

Magic! Twink caught her breath. But if it wasn't fairy magic, then what *was* it? Not many beings could perform magic.

'All right, you girls, get up to the school now,' bellowed a voice. Mrs Lightwing, the first-year head and Flight teacher, buzzed through the crowd. 'It's getting late – time to get settled into your branches, and then dinner!'

'But, Mrs Lightwing, what *is* that thing?' called a fourth-year fairy.

Unexpectedly, Mrs Lightwing gave her a brief smile, and patted her sky-blue hair into place. 'You'll find out tonight! Come on now, girls, flitter-flutter.' She skimmed back up the hill as the students looked at each other.

'*What* is going on?' murmured Pix.

'I don't know,' said Zena, a tall fairy from their branch. 'But I'm dying to find out!'

Shoving aside thoughts of the ice pole, Twink nudged Bimi's wing with her own. 'Come on,' she whispered. 'Let's make sure we get our usual beds!'

'Oh, I almost forgot,' gasped Bimi. 'Wasps, we'd better hurry!'

Their wings a-blur, the two fairies sped up the hill ahead of the others. Circling around the tree, they dived through the great double doors of Glitterwings.

Inside, the school was like a tall tower filled with golden light, with dozens of branches shooting off in all different directions from the main trunk. Fairies flitted in and out of them like humming-birds, as far up as the eye could see.

Twink and Bimi flew in quick spirals up the trunk, speeding past living branches and classrooms. About halfway up, they darted into a branch and landed with a hop at a bark doorway. A single yellow daffodil hung over the door.

'I think we're the first!' grinned Twink, breathing hard.

Bimi nodded, her eyes shining. 'Glimmery – we'll get our beds again!'

Twink pushed open the door. A long, cosy branch with green moss carpets and soft moss beds met her eyes, with a bright daffodil hanging over each one like a canopy. But Daffodil Branch wasn't empty after all. A fairy with lavender hair and pink wings lounged across one of the beds, reading a petal mag.

'Sooze!' Twink flitted into the branch with a startled laugh. Trust Sooze to be exactly where you didn't expect her!

Sooze jumped up. 'Hello, Opposite!' she cried, launching herself at Twink in a hug.

Twink had bright pink hair and lavender wings, the exact opposite of Sooze – hence the nickname.

'What are you doing here?' she asked as they pulled apart. 'Everyone else was down at the pond!'

Sooze raised an eyebrow. 'Why *shouldn't* I be here? I live here, remember? Hi, Bimi,' she added.

'Hi, Sooze,' smiled Bimi. 'Good hols?'

But Twink could see that a slight stiffness had come over her best friend. Bimi thought Sooze was irresponsible, and not to be depended on. Twink knew that she had a point – but Sooze could also be tremendous fun!

'Fantastic!' grinned Sooze now, flipping a strand

of lavender hair out of her eyes. 'We went to stay with my cousin – she goes to Sparklelight Academy, you know – and we got up to all sorts. We –'

'But, Sooze, didn't you see the ice pole?' interrupted Twink eagerly. 'It was so strange! It had these carvings all over it, and –'

Sooze shrugged. 'I saw it. It was really interesting, for about two wing beats. I don't know why everyone was so fascinated by a hunk of ice!'

Twink bit her lip in dismay. Sooze was never very interested in anything, unless it involved fast flying or playing pranks. The cold magic of the ice pole hadn't touched her at all.

'Come on, Twink, let's get our beds.' From the look on Bimi's face, Twink could tell she was thinking the same thing. She sighed inwardly. Oh, she wished that her two friends got along better!

'Your usual beds by the window?' Sooze fluttered her pink wings with a grin. 'I'm afraid that a very special someone has beaten you to them!'

Twink's jaw dropped. 'Who?'

'Mariella and Lola,' said Sooze, flopping on to her

bed again. 'Their things were already on them when I got here – have a look.'

Twink's heart sank as she saw that Sooze was right. Mariella's expensive wing polish sat smugly on the bedside mushroom that Twink had called her own for the last three terms. A drawing of Lola's family sat propped on Bimi's.

'The sneaky things!' burst out Twink. 'They must have flown up here before anyone else.'

Bimi looked disappointed, but merely lifted her wings. 'Well – that's what *we* were trying to do,' she pointed out reasonably.

'I know – but –' Twink stopped and made a face. If it had been anyone else, she wouldn't have minded so much. But that awful Mariella! It just wasn't fair.

Sooze's violet eyes sparkled. 'Let's move their things back to their usual beds! Just imagine Mosquito Nose's face when she comes back.' She glared down her nose, imitating Mariella.

Twink laughed despite herself. 'It's tempting – but no, we can't.'

'Let's take these two beds by the door,' suggested Bimi. 'They're just as nice, really – there's even an extra cupboard we can use.'

Twink sighed. 'I suppose you're right. I'll just miss being by the window, that's all.'

Taking the bed nearest the door, Twink started unpacking her petal bag. The other Daffodil Branch fairies began to flutter in, still buzzing excitedly about the ice pole. Mariella and Lola drifted in last of all. Mariella, a pointed-faced fairy with silvery-green hair, smirked broadly when she saw Twink.

'What's the matter?' she drawled, gazing from Twink to Bimi and back again. 'Didn't you two want your *usual* beds?' Lola, a thin little fairy with pale blue wings, giggled.

Twink tried to look surprised. 'No, we fancied a change. Did you want our old beds, then? You're welcome to them, if you like!'

Mariella flapped off with a scowl. Twink and Bimi grinned at each other. Taking her cricket clock out from its cage, Bimi patted the shiny brown creature on its head and fed it a bit of leaf.

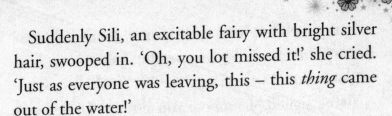

Suddenly Sili, an excitable fairy with bright silver hair, swooped in. 'Oh, you lot missed it!' she cried. 'Just as everyone was leaving, this – this *thing* came out of the water!'

Twink dropped her thistle comb on her bed. 'What thing?' she cried.

Sili waved her arms. 'Like – like a watery goblin! And it *talked*.' Sili deepened her voice. 'It said, *Treat the ice pole with respect! We have given it to you for a reason!*'

A baffled silence fell over the branch as the young fairies looked at each other.

Pix's forehead furrowed in thought. 'It must have been a water sprite,' she said. 'They're the only watery beings that have magic. But I didn't know that any lived in the school pond! They're very rare nowadays.'

A water sprite! Twink swallowed, remembering all the stories she had heard of the ill-tempered little creatures. She had only half-believed they were even real!

'But what did it mean?' wondered Bimi. '*What* reason?'

Zena shook her head. 'The school knows, though – remember what Mrs Lightwing said. We'll find out later, I guess.'

Mariella sniffed, and tossed her hair. 'Well, I think it's mean of them to keep us waiting like this. Our parents send us to school here. We've a right to know what's going on!'

Sooze rolled her eyes. 'Go and complain to Mummy, then. With any luck, she'll send you to school somewhere else!'

Mariella turned away with a flounce. Twink hid a smile – and then she forgot Mariella as she remembered the look on her parents' faces, and the gleaming carvings on the ice pole. Had Sili *really* seen a water sprite? Excitement thumped in her chest as she hastily finished unpacking.

Her father had said that she'd never forget this term, and Twink had a feeling he was right!

The Great Branch was the largest branch in the school – a long, high-ceilinged space filled with mossy green tables. A different flower hung over each one, so that in the summertime the Branch looked like a bright, sunny garden.

Now, in the heart of winter, the arched windows that lined the Branch were pitch-black, and the only light was from the pale glow-worm lanterns overhead. Twink caught her breath as she and Bimi flew into the Branch with the rest of the school. It was like a moonlit garden, shadowy and mysterious.

The two girls flitted to the Daffodil Branch table, perching on spotted mushroom seats. On the platform at the front of the Branch, Miss Shimmery, the HeadFairy, stood with her rainbow wings folded neatly behind her back. The year heads sat in a row behind her. From their faces, you'd think that nothing unusual was going on.

'I hope she doesn't make us wait too long,' Twink whispered to Bimi.

'I know,' Bimi whispered back. 'I can hardly wait to find out what's going on!'

When all the fairies were seated, Miss Shimmery flew gracefully up into the air. Instant silence fell over the Branch as several hundred young fairies turned towards her, eyes shining with anticipation.

'Welcome back to Glitterwings Academy, girls,' said Miss Shimmery in her low, strong voice. 'I trust that you all had a good Solstice holiday, and that you're rested and ready to begin a new term!'

Twink fidgeted on her mushroom. *Oh, please just tell us!* she implored silently. *We're all dying to know!*

The HeadFairy seemed to read her mind. A faint twinkle lit her eyes as she scanned her students. 'I have a very special announcement to make. You

Miss Shimmery

may have noticed a rather unusual addition to our school as you arrived – the ice pole in the pond.'

Yes! Twink sat up straight, heart pounding. She and Bimi exchanged a quick, eager glance.

'I will tell you all about it, but first, I must share with you something that not many fairies know,' said Miss Shimmery. 'The older years will be aware that we fairies help to change the seasons through our magic – but the exact means of this has always been kept secret, except for those fairies involved.'

Not a single wing moved in the Branch as the fairies listened.

'As you may know, spring begins at one exact spot every year, and then spreads outwards throughout the world,' went on Miss Shimmery. 'Changing winter into spring is one of the most important duties that a fairy can ever perform. The fairies who do so are chosen personally by Queen Mab.'

Miss Shimmery paused, looking out over the Branch. There was utter silence as the students gazed back at her, holding their breaths.

Finally a very small smile appeared on the

HeadFairy's face. 'I am proud to say that this year, Glitterwings Academy has the immense honour of having been chosen.'

A gasp rippled through the Branch. The Daffodil Branch table stared at each other, wide-eyed.

'But it is not only fairies who change winter to spring,' said Miss Shimmery. 'Other magical beings must help as well – and this year, the water sprites have agreed to take part. They are normally secretive creatures who keep to themselves, so we are doubly honoured.'

So it really *had* been a water sprite! Twink's eyes widened.

'The ice pole was built by the sprites,' went on Miss Shimmery. 'That is half of the magic. The other half will be provided by us. At dawn on the very last day of winter, every fairy in the school will take one of the icy strands of the ice pole and perform the sacred dance that weaves spring into being.'

Twink gripped the edges of her mushroom, her thoughts spinning in wonder. Miss Shimmery smiled as she hovered above them.

'Then, at just the right moment, we will use fairy dust to transform the pole into a green, growing thing. Spring will then begin, and will spread outwards from Glitterwings throughout the world.'

Fairy dust? But . . . they wouldn't learn how to use it until next year! Twink's throat went dry. Glancing around her, she saw the same worried look on the other First Years' faces. Were they not going to be allowed to take part?

Miss Shimmery's voice deepened. 'As I said, this is a very secret ceremony. The only fairies who will observe it will be us here at Glitterwings . . . and Queen Mab and her counsellors.'

For a moment the Great Branch didn't react, and then a quick intake of breath rippled through the room. *Queen Mab!* Here at Glitterwings! There was a low buzz of excited whispers.

Twink's eyes burned as she struggled to hold back tears. She had always longed to meet the beautiful and brave fairy queen. And now Queen Mab would actually be here, and she and her friends would have to sit on the sidelines! She swallowed hard, staring down at the gleaming wooden floor.

'I need hardly tell you that this is a once-in-a-life-time event,' said Miss Shimmery gravely. 'We want every student to be able to take part – and so the first-year students will be given the chance to learn how to use fairy dust this term. Those who master it will be included in the Spring Ceremony.'

Relief flooded through Twink like a mountain stream. She and Bimi squeezed hands, bouncing on their mushrooms. Across the table, Pix's eyes were shining like dewdrops. Even Mariella and Lola looked excited.

'That's all,' said Miss Shimmery with a smile. 'And now I think we should have a well-deserved meal. Butterflies commence!' She lifted an arm in the air as she drifted back down to the platform.

At her command, a rainbow of butterflies streamed into the Great Branch, carrying oak-leaf platters heaped high with seed cakes. They deposited the food on the tables with graceful flutters as the Great Branch burst into conversation.

'Just think!' gasped Sili. 'We'll be the fairies who

change winter into spring this year!'

'*If* we can learn how to use fairy dust.' A worried frown touched Bimi's face.

Pix laughed. 'Well, it can't be *too* hard – after all, Sooze's sister got the hang of it!'

'Flap off,' said Sooze with a grin. Her sister Winn was a fourth-year student at Glitterwings, and very like Sooze herself.

Twink swallowed a bite of seed cake. 'Sooze, has Winn ever said anything to you about how to use fairy dust?'

Sooze stared at her like she was mad. 'Why would we talk about *lessons*? We get enough of them at school! But I'm sure it's easy. All fairies can use fairy dust.' She poured herself some fresh dew from the almond-shell pitcher.

Twink bit her lip. All fairies could fly, too – but she hadn't been able to for ages. Would fairy dust cause her the same problems?

Bimi squeezed her hand. 'Don't worry,' she whispered. 'You'll be fine!'

Twink smiled gratefully at her. The best thing

about having a friend like Bimi was the way they could almost read each other's minds.

'So will you,' she murmured back. Bimi didn't have a very high opinion of her own cleverness at times, even though she had more common sense than any fairy Twink knew.

Bimi made a face. 'I hope so . . . I suppose we'll just have to see what happens.'

As the conversation buzzed at their table, Twink took another bite of seed cake, hardly tasting its sweetness. Her mind whirled with ice poles, water sprites and springtime.

Her father had been right. This term was going to be unforgettable!

Chapter Two

The Daffodil Branch fairies had never been so early for a lesson before. Long before Miss Sparkle was due to arrive at the Fairy Dust branch the next morning, Twink and the others were fluttering impatiently outside.

Now that school had started, they all wore matching daffodil dresses, with the Glitterwings oak-leaf cap perched on their heads. Other fairies flitted past on their way to class, wearing flower dresses that matched their own branches – poppies and bluebells and roses – all with the same jaunty oak-leaf cap.

Oh, it would be so glimmery to actually *use* fairy dust, instead of just talking about it! Twink bobbed in the air, unable to keep still. 'Just imagine turning winter into spring,' she breathed.

'And Queen Mab, here with all her counsellors!' added Sili. 'Why, we might even get to meet her.' She shot an inch or so up in the air at the thought.

Twink's heart raced. Meeting the Queen! Would it be possible?

Mariella tossed her silvery-green hair. 'My family is very well-known to the Queen. I'm sure *I'll* get to meet her!'

'Oh, Mariella, really?' breathed Lola as the others rolled their eyes.

'Of course,' said Mariella with a superior smile. 'I might even make sure you get to meet her, as well – if you learn how to use fairy dust, that is.'

'But *you* have to learn too, and you don't always do very well in your lessons, do you, Mosquito Nose?' said Sooze with a wicked gleam in her eye. 'I wouldn't be putting on airs just yet – you'll look pretty silly on the sidelines while the rest of us dance!'

Mariella's face darkened. Before she could respond, Miss Sparkle arrived.

'Hello, girls. You're a bit early, aren't you?' Unlocking the classroom door, she flitted into the branch. With a glare at Sooze, Mariella flounced off to sit at the back of the branch, with Lola close behind.

Twink perched on one of the spotted mushroom seats. She watched Miss Sparkle with shining eyes, determined to take in every word that the teacher said.

Miss Sparkle looked over her class with a wry expression. 'My, such a lot of eager students. I'm sure I've never seen you quite so keen before.' She folded her thin white wings behind her back. 'Well, shall we take some notes?'

Twink's face fell. *Notes?*

'But, Miss, we're supposed to learn how to use fairy dust!' cried Sili. 'Miss Shimmery said –'

Sili broke off as Miss Sparkle chuckled. The class

gaped at her. Miss Sparkle, *laughing*?

'In that case, perhaps we'd better have a look at this,' said Miss Sparkle. She unlocked the bark cupboard behind her desk.

Twink craned to see as their teacher took out a large oak-leaf bag and placed it on her mushroom podium. Fairy dust! She held her breath as Miss Sparkle scooped out a glittering handful. Bright pink and gold reflections danced through the branch as she turned her hand this way and that.

'We fairies perform magic in many ways,' said Miss Sparkle. 'With our singing, our dancing, and even our thoughts. Fairy dust is how we transform things – the most difficult magic of all.'

Suddenly Miss Sparkle tossed the fairy dust at a snail-trail pen on her desk. With a flash of golden light, the pen became a real snail, waving its antennae in confusion. The class gasped in delight.

Placing the snail on the podium, Miss Sparkle patted its shell. 'With the power to transform comes great responsibility. Can you imagine the chaos it would cause if a fairy were to use fairy dust carelessly? Or for a silly prank?' She gazed sternly at them.

Glancing at Sooze, Twink saw her friend sit up very straight, an expression of wide-eyed innocence on her face. Twink struggled to hold back a giggle. If she knew Sooze, she was already plotting!

'That's why we spend so long teaching you the *theory* of fairy dust before we allow you to use it,' continued Miss Sparkle. 'It's only to be used for the most sincere purposes.'

She tossed the remaining fairy dust on to the snail. Another flash of light lit the room as the snail became a pen again, falling to the podium with a clatter. The class sat very still, watching.

Miss Sparkle held up the pen and smiled. 'It looks easy, doesn't it? But there's a secret to using fairy dust. I can't tell you what it is; it's something every fairy must find out for herself. And until you do, you will never be able to use it.'

A secret? Twink's pink eyebrows drew together. Bimi, sitting on the mushroom beside her, looked more worried than ever.

'Pix, please pass out these rose petals.' Miss Sparkle held out a brightly coloured stack. As Pix flitted about the room, handing a rose petal to each of the girls, Miss Sparkle filled small bark boxes with fairy dust.

'This is your fairy dust,' she said, passing them out. 'You are not to take it out of this branch without my permission.'

Twink touched the side of her box, and then withdrew her fingers with a gasp. The fairy dust felt alive!

Fairy dust

Miss Sparkle returned to her podium. 'Let's begin. Your first assignment is to change your rose petal into a pixie boot.'

Twink looked doubtfully at the pink rose petal that Pix had laid on her desk. A pixie boot? It sounded awfully difficult for a first spell.

Miss Sparkle held up a glittering handful of dust, rubbing it between her fingers. 'Fairy dust is magic of *intent*. You must have the right intentions before its magic will work. If you do not, things can go terribly awry.'

She paused, scanning the class carefully. Twink swallowed hard. Now that the moment had come, she felt very unsure. Fairy dust sounded more dangerous than she had thought. What if she got it all wrong?

Finally Miss Sparkle nodded. 'You may open your boxes and take out a pinch of dust.'

Her heart thudding, Twink slowly creaked open the bark lid and reached inside her box.

'Oh,' she whispered. The pink and gold dust shimmered and sparkled, and seemed to tremble in her hand like nervous sand. She had never seen anything so beautiful!

Miss Sparkle cupped her hand. 'The throwing position is like so – hand cupped, fingers almost together. Remember, you are directing the fairy dust at the object, not scattering it to the winds.'

She fluttered about the room, correcting some of their holds. 'No, no, Pix – fingers too stiff; you need to relax. That's better. Mariella, you need to bend your elbow; you'll throw it right in Lola's face, holding it like that!' The class snickered as Mariella scowled.

Twink breathed a sigh of relief as Miss Sparkle nodded approval at her hold. 'Very nice, Twink. You too, Bimi. Fingers a bit more together. Now then,' she continued as she returned to the front of the branch. 'When you throw the dust, you *flick* outwards with your fingers.' She demonstrated with her hand. 'You see? *Flick!* Is everyone ready?'

Twink nodded with the others. Her stomach felt like a thousand anxious fleas were jumping about.

Miss Sparkle smiled. 'Some of your spells will

work instantly, and some will not. The reason why is the secret of fairy dust. Now, *concentrate* on what you wish to do. Think of all the reasons for it. What you think is very important!'

Twink closed her eyes tightly as she clutched the fairy dust. *I want to turn the petal into a pixie boot!* she thought. *I want to learn how to use fairy dust so I can dance in the Spring Ceremony!*

'– and THROW!'

Twink opened her eyes and flung the fairy dust at the petal. It sparkled in the air, making a noise like the tinkling of tiny chimes. She caught her breath. *Oh, please work!*

The fairy dust shimmered on the pink petal . . . and then faded. The petal hadn't changed. Twink bit her lip, wondering what she had done wrong. *Oh, well*, she thought. *I suppose it was silly of me to expect to get it first time.*

She glanced across at Bimi, ready to exchange rueful grins – and gasped in surprise. A perfect yellow pixie boot was sitting on Bimi's desk! Bimi stood staring at it with wide, disbelieving eyes.

'Bimi, you did it!' Twink flung an arm around her shoulders, hugging her hard. 'You clever thing!'

'But – but *how*?' gasped Bimi, laughing. 'I don't even know what I did!'

Miss Sparkle came over, beaming. 'Good work!' she said. 'Look, girls – Bimi's cracked it!'

The fairies clustered around, exclaiming excitedly. 'Oh, well done!' said Pix. 'I couldn't get mine to do a thing.'

'But I *haven't* cracked it!' Bimi's cheeks reddened. 'Honestly, Miss Sparkle – I don't know how I did it. I probably couldn't do it again.'

Miss Sparkle smiled. 'Well, let's see, shall we? Twink, hand me your petal. Now go on, Bimi, show us.' Miss Sparkle placed the petal on her desk.

Bimi looked red and flustered. Twink felt a pang of sympathy for her. She knew how much her friend hated being the centre of attention.

As everyone watched, Bimi reached into her bark box and took out another pinch of fairy dust. Shutting her eyes, she concentrated for a moment, and then tossed it at the petal.

With a shimmer of light, the petal became a pink pixie boot. The Daffodil Branch fairies burst into applause. Twink clapped harder than anyone – but at the same time, she couldn't help feeling just a tiny bit jealous. Bimi had changed the petal so easily!

'Oh, isn't it glimmery,' breathed Sili, picking up the pixie boot. 'Look, it even has a little bell on its toe!'

Miss Sparkle patted Bimi on the shoulder. 'I don't think you need to worry about not knowing the secret, Bimi. You *do* know, deep down – it's just part of who you are.'

Straightening her wings, Miss Sparkle looked around the branch. 'Is Bimi the only one who's got it?'

'No,' said a sulky voice. 'Lola's got it, too.'

Twink turned in surprise with the rest of the class to see Mariella glowering at Lola's mushroom desk. A bright red pixie boot sat on it. Lola's thin cheeks were flushed with pride.

Sooze burst out laughing. 'Glimmery, Lola! You'll have to teach Mariella how to do that, so she can impress the Queen.'

Miss Sparkle stilled the sniggers with a glance. 'Very good, Lola,' she said, inspecting the red pixie boot. 'Perfect work, in fact. I'm proud of you and Bimi both!'

'Thank you.' Lola's eyes shone as she smiled shyly at Miss Sparkle. Fuming at her side, Mariella looked like a volcano about to erupt.

Twink turned quickly away as laughter bubbled up inside her. Fancy Lola getting it and Mariella not!

Miss Sparkle glanced at the sun outside the window. 'Class is almost over,' she said. 'Please return any unused dust to your boxes, and write your names on the fronts.' She tapped her wings together, and gave Mariella a sharp-eyed look.

'And I know you're all keen to learn, but it's no good asking Bimi and Lola how they did it. Remember – the secret is something that you must find out for yourselves, or else it won't work!'

Chapter Three

Twink sat curled up on a window seat in the first-year Common Branch, gazing out of the window. Far below, through the bare winter branches, she could just see the frozen pond, with the glittering ice pole rising up from the centre of it.

She sighed, and slumped her chin on her hand. It had been weeks and weeks now since Miss Sparkle had first let them use fairy dust, but Twink just couldn't seem to get the hang of it. Her petals stayed petals, no matter what she tried.

And to make matters worse, more than half the

first year had got the secret by now, with new fairies succeeding every day. In Daffodil Branch, both Sili and Zena had got it. Twink was terrified that the rest of Daffodil Branch would work it out too, one by one, until she was the only one left who didn't have a clue.

Oh, how could she bear it if she wasn't one of the ones dancing about the ice pole when Queen Mab came? She'd never have another chance in her life to change winter into spring!

Suddenly a fourth-year fairy with purple hair flitted past the window. 'Six hundred and two, six hundred and three . . .' Her voice faded as she flew off. Another Fourth Year followed, busily writing something on a petal pad.

Twink opened the window and leaned out. 'What are you doing?' she called.

'Counting the twigs on the branches, to see how many ice ornaments we'll need for Queen Mab's visit,' the fairy called back. 'We're doing one for each of them!'

Twink perked up. Ice ornaments sounded

glimmery! 'Can First Years help?' she asked eagerly.

'Of course!' said the fairy. 'So long as you can use fairy dust, anyone can!'

She flew off. Twink groaned and banged the window shut. Fairy dust again! How could she ever have been so excited by it? She was starting to dread even going to the class now.

Twink glanced across the Common Branch. Pix sat at one of the mushroom desks, her yellow wings slumping as she pored over a pile of thick petal books. *Fairy Dust Through the Ages, A Concise History of Fairy Dust, Fairy Dust Spells.* As Twink watched, Pix sighed and turned a page.

Twink made a sympathetic face. Pix hadn't worked the secret out either, and it was driving her mad! She was used to being the clever one who knew all the answers. But it seemed as if the secret to fairy dust had nothing to do with being clever.

'Hi,' said Bimi, sliding on to the window seat beside Twink.

'Hi.' Twink moved her legs to make room for her friend.

Bimi's blue eyes were concerned. 'Oh, Twink, please don't worry! You'll get it soon, I know you will.'

'I may not get it in time for the ceremony, though. It's only two weeks away now.' Twink drew her knees up to her chin and gazed out of the window again. She knew Bimi was only trying to help, but she didn't feel like being cheered up.

'I bet you will,' said Bimi. 'We'll do the dance together, wait and see!'

'How do you know?' said Twink irritably. 'Fairy

dust doesn't come naturally to me the way it does to you.' Her voice came out crosser than she had intended.

'I wish it didn't!' burst out Bimi. Her silver and gold wings fluttered with agitation. 'It's awful being able to use fairy dust when you can't.'

'Bimi, don't be silly!' said Twink, startled out of her mood. 'You'll get to change winter into spring! And the Queen will be there, and –'

Bimi's shoulders slumped. 'Yes, but it won't be any fun if you can't do it too. How could I enjoy it, knowing that you're so sad?'

Twink instantly felt guilty. She sat up and rubbed her wing against Bimi's. 'I won't be sad, I'll be cheering you on!' she said warmly. 'I think it's wonderful that you got it so quickly, Bimi. If I can't dance around the ice pole myself, having you do it will be the next best thing.'

Bimi looked hopeful. 'Really? You wouldn't hate me for it?'

'Of course not!' Twink assured her. 'And who knows – maybe I'll get the secret in time after all.'

Inwardly, though, she sighed. How was she ever going to get the secret when she had no idea what she was doing wrong?

'I wish I could help you,' said Bimi softly, reading her mind as usual. 'I mean, I know Miss Sparkle told us not to tell, but if I knew how I did it I could at least try to steer you in the right direction.'

'I know,' said Twink, leaning back against the window. It was getting dark outside, and the glass felt chilly against her wings. 'I'll just have to get it on my own, somehow.'

Sooze, who had been fluttering restlessly about the branch for the last half hour, flitted over to them. 'And what are *you* two talking about?' she demanded grumpily. She held up a hand before Twink could answer. 'No, wait! Let me guess! *Fairy dust!*'

Twink laughed despite herself. 'Fairy dust,' she admitted. 'What of it?'

Sooze rolled her eyes. 'You and everyone else in this branch! Fairy dust, fairy dust – that's all *anyone* talks about these days.'

Bimi lifted her shoulder coolly. 'I suppose everyone wants to dance in the ceremony, that's all.'

Sooze blew a strand of lavender hair from her face. 'Well, I do too, but not if it means I have to practise fairy dust until my wings fall off. I'm sick of trying to work it out!'

She propped her hands on her hips, glancing around the Common Branch with a scowl. 'Everyone's acting so serious and gloomy. We need to do something to liven things up!'

Twink grinned. Maybe Bimi wasn't thrilled to see Sooze, but she herself felt better already. 'Liven things up? Like what?'

A mischevious glint flashed in Sooze's eyes. She propped a finger on her chin. 'We-ell, now that you mention it . . . it's been an *awfully* long time since we've played a prank, hasn't it?'

Bimi's mouth tightened. 'A prank? With Queen Mab coming soon?'

Sooze's wings flashed as she darted away, laughing. 'Oh, don't worry, I won't involve the two of you!' she called over her shoulder. 'But something

definitely needs to be done!'

Twink and Bimi looked at each other as Sooze disappeared out of the door. 'What do you think she's going to do?' asked Bimi. She sounded half intrigued and half disapproving.

Twink shrugged. 'Who can tell!' she said happily. 'But knowing Sooze, it's sure to be interesting.'

Sooze spiralled quickly down the great trunk, enjoying the wind singing through her wings. Glancing around to see whether any year heads were about, she abandoned her spirals and plunged into a steep dive, her lavender hair streaming out behind her. Glimmery! She loved flying fast, even though it wasn't allowed inside the school.

With a quick midair somersault, Sooze dipped off to a branch on the left. Landing neatly in front of a red doorway, she edged open the door and slipped inside. The fourth-year Common Branch was long and cheerful-looking, with clusters of shiny mushroom desks and cosy sitting areas.

'Is Winn here?' called Sooze.

A crowd of fourth-year students looked up. 'No First Years allowed!' snapped a fairy with bright yellow hair. 'What do you mean, barging in here?'

Sooze grinned, not daunted in the slightest. 'I'm just looking for my sister, that's all.' She flitted up towards the ceiling. 'Winn!' she shouted, spotting her sister at the other end of the branch. 'I need to talk to you!'

The yellow-haired fairy darted into the air, grabbing her arm. 'Out!' she said grimly. 'You First Years are too cheeky for words. In my day, we had some respect for the older years!'

Sooze started to answer back, but thought better of it. Fourth-year students could give the younger years detention if they thought it necessary – and that wouldn't fit in with Sooze's plans at all. 'Sorry,' she said cheerfully.

Winn came flying up, her face a scowl. 'Sooze, you little wasp brain! What do you think you're doing?'

'You need to teach your sister some manners,' said the yellow-haired fairy crossly. She shoved Sooze towards her.

Winn rolled her eyes. 'Oh, we've all tried; she's impossible. Come on, Sooze, let's go outside.'

Winn looked very much like her sister, with the same lavender hair and pink wings. Normally they shared the same laughing expression as well, but now Winn just looked annoyed.

The two sisters flew out of the branch and hovered in the trunk. 'Now, what's up?' demanded Winn. 'You'd better have a good reason for barging into our Common Branch!'

'Of course,' grinned Sooze. Quickly, she explained what she had in mind. Once she had finished, Winn smiled despite herself.

'You little scamp! But I bet you're right – half the first year must be miserable, thinking they may not get to dance in the ceremony. A prank could be just the thing.'

Sooze nodded eagerly. 'And we haven't played one on Madame in absolutely ages! You'll help, won't you?'

Winn hesitated. It wouldn't be the first time that

she had helped her sister out with a prank – but everyone was so serious at the moment, with the Queen coming soon! Maybe it wasn't a good idea.

'Please!' wheedled Sooze. 'Just imagine the look on Madame's face!'

A mischievous sparkle lit Winn's eyes. The thought of Madame's reaction was too delicious to resist!

'All right,' she decided. 'Meet me by the front doors straight after breakfast tomorrow. That'll give you time to set things up before your Dance class.'

'Hurrah!' Sooze darted into her sister's arms and hugged her tightly. 'You're the best sister in the world!'

Winn laughed and pushed her away. 'Yes, I know! Go to bed now, before Mrs Lightwing catches you here.'

Chapter Four

Twink sat perched on her mossy bed, carefully polishing her wings. First she poured a dollop of dandelion milk on to her hands from a tiny bottle, gently smoothing it on to her wings from tip to tail. Then she gave them a brisk rub-down with a rose petal, so that they gleamed like pink gemstones.

Sitting on the next bed, Bimi was busy working a thistle comb through her long blue hair. All the other Daffodil Branch fairies were getting ready for bed, too, but the branch was oddly silent, with none of its usual laughter and chatter. Twink sighed.

Everyone was too worked up about fairy dust to feel like laughing.

And where was Sooze? She glanced anxiously at Sooze's empty bed. Mrs Hover, the matron, would be coming in at any moment!

Just then Sooze flitted into the branch, humming to herself. 'Hello, everyone!' she sang. She did a midair somersault, landing with a flourish in the centre of the room. The daffodil blossoms that hung over every bed bounced wildly in the sudden breeze.

'Why are *you* in such a good mood?' demanded Sili with a grin.

Sooze winked at her. 'Oh, no reason!' Still humming, she danced to her bed and started to undress.

'You're up to something,' said Pix suspiciously. The clever fairy looked tired and cross. Weeks of trying to work out the riddle of fairy dust hadn't left her in a very good mood.

'Me?' Sooze widened her eyes. 'Don't be silly. Come on, we have to get ready for bed before Mrs Hover gets here. Look at your wings, they're not even polished yet!'

Pix blew out an irritated breath and turned away. 'Fine, have it your way!'

The branch went quiet again as everyone returned to their bedtime tasks – except for Sooze's humming, which warbled through the silence like a nightingale. Twink and Bimi looked at each other.

'She *is* up to something,' whispered Bimi.

Twink nodded, her pulse quickening. 'She must have worked out a prank already!'

Bimi put down her comb. 'I'm not sure she should, you know. Not *now*, with the Queen coming!'

The sensible part of Twink agreed with her – but another part could hardly wait to see what Sooze was up to! 'I know,' she whispered back. 'But we can't stop her, so we might as well just enjoy it.'

Bimi glanced across the branch, and then leaned close to Twink. 'Anyway, she's not the only one who's up to something. Look at Mariella!'

Looking across to their old beds, Twink saw that Mariella and Lola had moved them closer to the

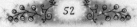

windows, so that they were slightly apart from the rest of the branch. Mariella sat on the edge of her bed, whispering fiercely to Lola. Lola sat limply on her own bed, staring at the floor.

Twink's lips tightened. 'She's trying to get Lola to tell her the secret of fairy dust!'

Bimi nodded, her blue eyes concerned. 'It's been weeks now – I can't believe Lola hasn't told her already. She must be made of stronger stuff than we thought.'

All at once a green pixie boot flew through the air,

hitting Mariella squarely on the nose. 'Oh!' she shrieked, jumping up. 'Who did that?'

'I did!' snapped Pix, propping her hands on her hips. 'Just leave her alone, can't you? If you can't work out fairy dust on your own, it serves you right!'

Mariella's pointed face flushed dark red. 'Who says I'm trying to get her to tell me anything? I'm not, Lola, am I?'

Lola looked like a moth caught in a flame. 'Oh – um – no, no she isn't,' she stammered. 'We were just chatting, that's all.'

'Anyway, you're a fine one to talk, Pix!' continued Mariella, tossing her silvery-green hair. 'Not so clever now, are you? Haven't you found the secret in one of your books yet?'

'You can't find it in books!' burst out Zena. She had worked out the secret a week or so after Bimi. 'You have to just *feel* it – and if it's what I think it is, Mariella, I can tell you right now that *you'll* never feel it in a million years!'

The branch stared at her. Zena, who was normally

so calm and quiet! But now the tall fairy's face was flushed, her orange wings trembling with anger.

Mariella went pale. 'How dare you! Why –'

'Girls! *What* is going on?' The branch went quiet as Mrs Hover bustled in, huffing from her long flight up the trunk. 'Bickering like babies in an acorn nursery! You should all be ashamed. Now, into bed. I don't want to hear another word. Glow-worms out!'

Climbing into bed, Twink pulled her petal duvet up around her pointed ears. As she listened to the angry silence all around her, she thought that Sooze's prank couldn't come too soon. If *something* didn't lighten the mood before long, they'd all be at each other's wings!

After breakfast the next morning, Sooze skimmed lightly over the frozen grass, clutching the petal-wrapped packet that Winn had just given her. The day was cold and grey, but her heart sang as though it was flooded with sunshine. Oh, this was going to be such fun!

But when she got to the ring of enchanted mushrooms where their Dance class usually took place, there was a notice written on an oak leaf:

Dance class will take place beside the pond this morning. Please be prompt.
                                            Madame Brightfoot

By the pond? Sooze thought of the ice pole, and hesitated. Water sprites were such cross, secretive little creatures. They might not appreciate having a prank played beside their precious pole! Maybe she should save it for another time.

Then she blew out an impatient breath. Oh, she had got just as bad as the others! The ice pole was just a chunk of carved ice, that was all. And the prank really was too good to save.

Flying at top speed, Sooze darted around the tree and down the small hill to the pond. The ice pole rose up from its frozen centre, its long, icy strands chiming together in the breeze.

Sooze landed on the edge of the pond and quickly

unfolded the petal. A single perfect snowflake lay inside, about half the size of her hand, enchanted so that it wouldn't melt. She held it up, admiring its lacy delicacy, and then placed it carefully on a pebble.

The prank was very simple. The snowflake would wait on its pebble until class began. Then, when Sooze whispered the magic words under her breath, it would drift up into the air and land on the tip of Madame's nose – and that's exactly where it would stay, no matter what Madame did!

Sooze giggled, imagining the look on Madame's face when she discovered she had a snowflake she couldn't get rid of. This was going to be glimmery!

What were the magic words, though? Oh, wasps! She hadn't forgotten them already, had she? Sooze's lavender eyebrows came together as she tried to remember.

'*Snowflake rise, snowflake blow . . . snowflake land upon her nose,*' she muttered. No, that wasn't it. '*Snowflake rise, snowflake go . . . snowflake fly on to her nose.*'

On the pebble, the snowflake shuddered suddenly. Too wrapped up in her thoughts to notice, Sooze continued. '*Snowflake fly, snowflake blow . . . go right now and find a nose!*'

The snowflake burst off the pebble in a rush, *zinging* past Sooze's ear. She yelped, and then gasped in horror as she realised what she had done. *How* could she have been so stupid?

The snowflake was buzzing about the pond like a deranged fly, faster and faster. 'No!' called Sooze, waving her arms. 'It's not time yet!'

The snowflake took no notice. Its circles became smaller, until it was zipping about the ice pole itself, dangerously close to its carved creatures. Sooze gave a squeak and took off after it. 'No! Come back!'

She darted about wildly as she chased it, trying to guess which way it would go next. 'Oh, *stop!*' she cried, close to tears.

Shining like a white dragonfly, the snowflake jetted to the very top of the pole and crashed right into it. A robin's carved beak broke off with a resounding *snap,* and fell on to the ice with a

tiny tinkling noise.

Sooze's hands flew to her mouth in horror. 'Oh, no,' she whispered.

Slowly, she flew down and picked up the beak. It stayed cold and hard in her hand, enchanted like the snowflake.

What on earth was she going to do? Clutching the beak, Sooze looked at the top of the pole. She could see the beak-less robin perched there, looking very silly indeed. The snowflake, now an ordinary snowflake once again, drifted gently to the ground.

Crash!

Sooze screamed as a section of the frozen pond burst outwards, sending ice shards flying in all directions. A small green head popped through the hole. A pair of round, water-coloured eyes glared at Sooze.

'What is the meaning of this!' demanded the water sprite.

Sooze gulped, and whisked the beak behind her back. 'I – I was just playing a prank. I didn't mean –'

'A prank!' screeched the creature. Its eyes bulged like an angry frog. 'A prank that has ruined our ice pole! Bah – you fairies have no respect! It is always the same with you! Pranks, and fun, and no respect for beautiful ice poles!'

'No!' cried Sooze. 'I mean – I mean, most fairies have a lot of respect for it! I didn't mean to break it, I really didn't. You can mend it, can't you?' She held her breath.

The water sprite snorted in derision. 'We can, but we shall not!'

'But – but you have to,' faltered Sooze. 'The ceremony – we have to change winter into spring –'

'You must mend it yourself, you stupid fairy – you, and no one else! Or we shall take away the ice pole and no one will use it at all. Bah! We should have known better than to trust the fairies!'

With a furious splash, the water sprite dived back under the water. 'Wait!' called Sooze, her wings fluttering in alarm. 'I don't know how to mend it! Does it just attach back on? What do I do?'

But there was no answer. The hole froze quickly

over again, until there was no sign the sprite had been there at all. Spurred by sudden panic, Sooze flitted to the top of the pole and tried to press the beak on to the robin's face. It fell off in her hand.

Licking her finger, Sooze frantically wet the end of the beak and tried again. 'Please, please work!' she muttered. But the beak refused to stay attached.

'Sooze, what are you doing?' called a voice.

Sooze gasped. Twink and the others were flying towards her in a brightly coloured stream. It was time for class! Quickly slipping the beak into her

pocket, Sooze flew to the bank and tried to look relaxed.

Twink landed lightly beside Sooze, eyes gleaming. 'Is it the prank?' she whispered.

Sooze flinched. 'I – no – sort of,' she muttered, cheeks blazing. 'Just forget the prank, Twink!'

Twink's face fell. 'But I thought you were going to play one. Everyone's in such a bad mood –'

'Oh, who cares!' burst out Sooze. 'It's not up to *me* to cheer them up, is it?' She turned quickly away as the others arrived, not wanting to see the hurt look on Twink's face.

Madame Brightfoot fluttered grandly down into their midst. Her rich purple hair was piled atop her head, and her red wings shone against the grey day.

'Flower Formation, everyone!' she cried. Her cobweb dress shimmered as she waved her arms about. 'Quickly, quickly!'

Glumly, Sooze got into position with the others, holding hands with the fairies on either side of her. Once they were all in a circle, they opened their wings so that the very tips of them touched. From above, they looked like a many-petalled flower.

Madame nodded in approval. 'Very nice. We shall now do a thank-you dance to the sprites for their ice pole – and once we have finished, I am sure that they will appear in response!'

The blood left Sooze's face. Oh, no! Would the sprites appear and tell everyone what she had done? Woodenly, she tried to follow Madame's steps as the dance began.

'And *sway* to the left . . . spin once, twice, three times! Now, up in the air! Think thank-you thoughts!' Madame hovered in the centre of the circle, waving her arms in time to the dance.

Sooze's wings felt clammy. What on earth could she say? *Um . . . thank you for the ice pole,* she thought timidly. *It was really glimmery until I broke it.* Oh, that didn't sound right at all!

'Now land,' said Madame finally. The fairies drifted to the ground. Beaming broadly, Madame cocked an ear at the pond. 'Any moment now,' she whispered.

Sooze nibbled her thumb. The pond's icy surface

stayed still and silent.

Madame's purple eyebrows drew together. 'How odd!' She straightened abruptly. 'We shall try the dance again! Someone wasn't thinking hard enough! Come now, quickly!'

This time when they finished the dance, Madame got on her hands and knees, cupping a hand about her ear as she listened. 'But I do not understand!' she murmured. 'I am sure we did the dance perfectly.' She looked up at the ice pole, frowning in puzzlement.

Sooze stifled a yelp. She might see the broken robin! 'Please, Madame – I think they're just tired!' she blurted.

Madame stared at her. '*Tired?* What do you mean?'

Sooze swallowed. 'I – I was down here before class started, and I saw one of them. He said they're tired of all the attention they've got since they built the pole – they just want to be left alone.'

She saw the class glance at each other, wondering if this was part of a prank, or for real! Madame

tapped her wings together. 'Is this true, Sooze?'

'Oh, yes!' said Sooze. The broken beak felt sharp in her pocket, and she hurried on, 'I mean – well, why else wouldn't they appear when we danced?'

Madame nodded slowly. 'Yes . . . yes, I suppose so. Well, then – in that case we shall simply do a silent dance of respect. Follow me, girls.'

As the class imitated Madame's moves, Sooze let out a breath. She had got away with it – for now, at least!

But what would happen if she couldn't mend the robin's beak? Sooze gulped, remembering what the sprite had said. The Spring Ceremony would be cancelled – and it would be all her fault.

No! she thought desperately. *I'll mend it somehow. I will!*

Chapter Five

Twink stood in a long line with the other first-year fairies, trying not to look bored as Mrs Lightwing flew up and down in front of them in the moonlight.

'I've been seeing some very sloppy wingwork from you girls lately! Don't think that just because the Spring Ceremony is only a few days away that you can neglect your flying lessons.' Mrs Lightwing stopped and hovered, fixing them all with a stern stare.

Twink held back a sigh. Night Flying had

sounded so exciting on her timetable this term – but it had turned out to be just like Flight, only at night!

Mrs Lightwing's sensible oak-leaf dress rustled in the evening breeze. 'Flying teams, please!' she barked. 'We're going to do some exercises.'

As Twink flitted into place with Pix and Bimi, she glanced at Sooze, who was on a team with Sili and Zena. Her friend was flying with her head down, looking nothing at all like her usual sparkly self.

Twink frowned. *What* was wrong with Sooze? She had been acting odd for days. Only yesterday, Twink had caught her sneaking a bit of sap glue out of the supplies branch. When Twink had asked her about it, Sooze had just mumbled something and flown quickly away.

Maybe it was for a prank, thought Twink hopefully. But it was over a week ago now that Sooze had mentioned a prank. Now it seemed to be the last thing on her mind.

'Full speed, three left-sided barrel rolls on my command, and then a loop-the-loop,' announced

Mrs Lightwing. 'And any fairy with sloppy wing-work will find herself doing laps around the school!'

Mariella tossed her head. 'Oh, I could do that in my sleep,' she said in a piercing whisper. 'But then, I *am* a very advanced flier.'

Twink rolled her eyes and glanced expectantly at Sooze. Sooze loved it when Mariella came out with her snooty remarks – it gave her an excuse to respond with cutting comments of her own!

But Sooze didn't seem to have heard. She was hovering a little way apart from Sili and Zena, staring towards the pond.

Maybe she's thinking of the ceremony, thought Twink. Sooze still hadn't worked out fairy dust.

Neither had Twink, and she sighed. She didn't suppose she'd be dancing in the ceremony now. She thought wistfully of Queen Mab, and how she had hoped to meet her. The Queen would hardly want to meet a fairy who couldn't even use fairy dust.

Twink frowned. But *Sooze* wasn't the sort to mope about a thing like that. What on earth could be wrong with her?

Mrs Lightwing raised her arm and dropped it. 'First team – go!' A team from Poppy Branch jetted off into the night, their red dresses flashing.

Leaning close to Bimi and Pix, Twink whispered, 'Have you two noticed anything strange about Sooze recently?'

'Strange how?' Bimi whispered back.

Twink shrugged, unsure how to express it. 'She just doesn't seem very happy, that's all.' She thought about the sap glue, but decided against mentioning it.

'She's probably just down because she hasn't got the hang of fairy dust yet,' said Pix. Pix had worked out the secret only a few days before, to her immense relief. Afterwards, she'd looked almost sheepish as she said, 'Zena was right, you know – it's not something you can find in books!'

'Second team,' called Mrs Lightwing. Mariella and Lola skimmed away.

Twink shook her head. 'No, I don't think that's it. Sooze wants to dance in the ceremony, but she doesn't care about it *that* much. I think something might really be wrong.'

'With Sooze?' Bimi looked surprised. 'What could be wrong?'

'I don't know,' said Twink. 'But –'

'Look out!' shrieked several fairies.

Twink spun round, and gasped. Mariella wasn't watching where she was going – and she was about to fly straight into a large brown moth!

Crash! Twink winced as Mariella and the moth collided in a flurry of wings. 'Oh!' screeched Mariella, struggling to disentangle herself. 'Get off

70

me! You clumsy – stupid –'

Well, thought Twink, she obviously wasn't hurt, with the fuss she was making! Twink held back a wild giggle as Mariella spluttered and shouted, all flailing legs and flapping wings. Lola fluttered about them helplessly, tugging at first one and then the other.

'Brilliant!' whispered Pix. 'And after she was just bragging about her flying, as well!'

Mrs Lightwing flew up, grim-faced. With a single wrench of her hand, she had the moth separated from Mariella and zigzagging dazedly on its way.

'Oh! Did you see that clumsy thing!' shrieked Mariella, stamping her foot in the air. 'It just crashed straight into me! It . . .' She trailed off, noticing for the first time the expression on Mrs Lightwing's face.

'*What* is the rule about right of way with moths, Mariella?' demanded their Flight teacher.

Mariella paled. 'Er . . . pass on the left,' she said weakly.

'PASS ON THE LEFT!' boomed Mrs Lightwing.

'NOT try to go straight through them!'

Twink quickly pressed her hand over her mouth to hold in her laughter. She knew she shouldn't, but – oh, dear! Mariella deserved it!

Mariella scowled. 'Yes, but –'

'But nothing!' snapped Mrs Lightwing. 'That was the WORST bit of flying I have ever seen. You could have seriously injured that poor moth!'

'Injured *him*?' burst out Mariella. 'What about me?'

'You deserve what you get,' said Mrs Lightwing grimly. 'Now, thirty laps around the school – go on!'

'But that's not fair! He –'

'*Fifty* laps – do you want to make it more?' Mrs Lightwing folded her arms across her chest.

Mariella fell into an angry silence, glaring at the dark ground. Mrs Lightwing jerked her head towards the school. 'Go on, then – start flying!' Mariella buzzed off towards Glitterwings, looking ready to explode.

Grinning to herself, Twink glanced at Bimi and Pix. Bimi's blue eyes were sparkling with suppressed giggles, while Pix was almost doubled over in the air, struggling to hold in howls of laughter. The rest of Daffodil Branch was in much the same state. The other first-year fairies might find Mariella a pain during Flight lessons, but Daffy Branch had to live with her all the time! It was glimmery to see her get her come-uppance so firmly for once.

Mrs Lightwing shook her sky-blue head. 'Lola, join the next team, please. Now, let's continue – third team!'

Twink caught sight of Sooze, and her merriment faded. Sooze wasn't even smiling. As Twink watched, she glanced worriedly at the pond again.

'Look!' hissed Twink, nudging her friends. 'I told you something was wrong. Sooze doesn't even care that Mariella just got told off!'

Bimi and Pix stared at Sooze, their eyes wide. 'Oh,' whispered Bimi. 'Twink, I think you're right – something must really be wrong!'

At dinner that night, Sooze sat at the end of the Daffodil Branch table, apart from the others. Twink looked anxiously at her. She had tried to talk to Sooze after the Flight class, but Sooze had vehemently insisted that nothing was wrong. Now she looked glummer than ever, picking listlessly at her food.

Suddenly Sili leaned across the table, her long silver hair almost touching the oak-leaf platter of seed cakes. 'Have you three noticed that Sooze is acting strange?' she hissed.

Twink nodded. 'We were talking about it earlier,' she whispered back.

'What do you think's wrong with her?' asked Bimi.

Sili shook her head, her large eyes wider than ever. 'Zena and I can't work it out. She's acting like – like she's committed some terrible crime!'

Bimi clapped her wings together impatiently. 'Oh, don't be silly. Of course she hasn't!'

'But she's obviously upset about something,' whispered Pix. 'And if she doesn't want to talk about it, I wonder if we can't cheer her up, somehow?'

'We could have a fairy cabaret!' squealed Sili

softly, bouncing on her mushroom seat. 'We could all sing a song, or do a dance, or –'

Twink shook her head, remembering how Sooze hadn't even smiled when Mariella got told off. 'I don't think that would work, Sili.'

'What are you lot talking about?' demanded Mariella. The pointed-faced fairy's eyes were narrowed as she watched them from the end of the table.

Sili giggled and flipped her hair back. 'You, actually! We were saying how fit you must be after all those laps.'

Sniffing loudly, Mariella turned away. A moment later she was whispering in Lola's ear, and Lola was squirming uncomfortably. 'I *can't*, Mariella,' Twink heard her mumble.

Twink shook her head in disgust. Why couldn't Mariella just work the secret out on her own, like everybody else?

Pix tapped a bit of seed cake against her oak-leaf plate. 'Maybe I can find a reference in the library that would help us cheer Sooze up. Or we could try

a daisy mood-altering charm – if we can find all the ingredients in the Flower Power cupboard, of course –'

Bimi shrugged. 'I think we should just be really nice to her,' she said. 'And if she wants to tell us what's wrong, she will.'

Pix blinked. 'Or . . . yeah,' she said lamely. 'We could just do that, I suppose.'

With a swooping rustle, the school's butterflies fluttered into the Great Branch to clear away the remains of dinner. As she got up with the rest of the

Daffodil Branch table, Twink saw Bimi flit across to Sooze's side.

'I saved you a bit of seed cake,' she said brightly. 'It's your favourite, isn't it?'

Twink's heart swelled with pride as she watched her best friend. Bimi didn't even like Sooze very much, but she was trying so hard to help her! It didn't even occur to her not to. That was just the sort of fairy she was.

Suddenly Twink gasped and stopped short. *Of course!* she thought, her mouth falling open. That was it!

She knew the secret of fairy dust.

Chapter Six

Twink sat impatiently at her mushroom desk, waiting for Miss Sparkle to pass out the boxes of fairy dust. Oh, why wouldn't she hurry!

Bimi raised her eyebrows. 'What's wrong? You seem all . . . twitchy.'

Twink hesitated, and then shook her head. 'Nothing. I just want to get started, that's all.' Normally she told Bimi everything, but her confidence had taken a knock after weeks of trying to work out the secret. If she was wrong, she'd rather keep it to herself!

Miss Sparkle put Twink's bark box on her desk and handed her a fresh rose petal. Twink's spine tingled as she looked at it. Would it be a boot soon? Or just stay a petal, like all the rest?

'Those of you who know how to use fairy dust, please try the spell I've written on the barkboard,' said Miss Sparkle. 'The rest of you, keep trying. Don't worry, you've still plenty of time.'

Miss Sparkle's smile was encouraging, but Twink wasn't at all sure she really meant what she said. The ceremony was only two days away now!

Slowly, Twink opened her box. The fairy dust gave off pink and golden sparks as she scooped out a shimmering handful.

Beside her, Bimi was carefully reading the spell on the barkboard, preparing to change a pebble into a woodlouse. For the more advanced fairy dust magic you had to use spells – and some of them were very tricky.

Twink turned back to her petal and took a deep breath. It was time to test out her theory. She mustn't think of the reasons why *she* wanted the dust to work – instead, she needed to focus on how she could help others with it.

Squeezing the dust against her palm, she closed her eyes. *Please let me change this petal into a boot, so that someone who doesn't have a shoe can wear it – and so that I can help to bring in the spring for the whole world!*

She repeated the words over and over, meaning them with her whole heart. She felt her hand begin to tingle. Opening her eyes, Twink quickly threw the fairy dust on to the petal.

There was a noiseless flash of pink and golden light. A purple-red pixie boot sat on Twink's desk, perfect in every detail – even down to the tiny bell at its toe!

'Oh!' cried Twink. 'I did it, I did it!'

Bimi shrieked and clutched her arm, bouncing up and down. 'Twink! You clever thing! Oh, I'm so glad!' Her face was alight with happiness – in fact, Twink thought she looked happier than when she herself had worked it out!

'Hurrah!' cried Sili, bounding across the branch to hug her.

Pix grinned. 'Well done! I knew you could do it, Twink.'

Miss Sparkle flitted over, beaming broadly. 'Oh, good work, Twink!' She picked up the pixie boot, turning it over in her hands. 'Yes, perfect! You've got it now, haven't you?' Her dark eyes smiled into Twink's.

'Yes, I – I think so,' said Twink. Her heart was singing.

Miss Sparkle handed the boot back to Twink and patted her shoulder. 'Yes, that's the thing about fairy dust. Once you know the secret it becomes a part of you for ever, making you a better fairy. Well done.'

Twink nodded slowly as a warm glow spread through her. Miss Sparkle was right. Of course she was glad for herself that she wouldn't be left out of the Spring Ceremony – but suddenly that didn't matter nearly as much as being able to help turn winter into spring. And the funny thing was that the secret was so simple! Why hadn't she realised it ages ago?

'Excuse me, Miss!' announced a haughty voice.

Mariella smirked as everyone turned towards her. 'I've got it, too.' A yellow pixie boot sat on her desk, looking every bit as perfect as Twink's.

Miss Sparkle lifted her eyebrows with a surprised smile. 'Mariella! Well done!'

Flitting to the back of the branch, she picked up Mariella's pixie boot – but no sooner had she touched it than it fell to pieces in her hands. Mariella gasped in dismay as the petals drifted to the floor.

Miss Sparkle shook her head sternly. 'Mariella, you didn't find the secret out for yourself, did you?'

Mariella flushed. 'Of course I did!'

Miss Sparkle looked at Lola. The thin little fairy gulped. 'I – I just gave her a hint,' she whispered.

'That's what friends are for, isn't it? Mariella said . . .' She trailed off, her pale wings slumping miserably.

Miss Sparkle frowned, and turned back to Mariella. 'I thought so,' she said. 'You can always tell when someone hasn't worked fairy dust out for themselves. You have to really *feel* the secret, Mariella.

Until you do, your spells will always be shoddy things that don't work.'

Mariella's face was on fire as Miss Sparkle turned away. Twink and Bimi exchanged a look. Trust Mariella to cheat – it served her right to have been caught out!

'Sooze, how are you doing?' Miss Sparkle's eyes widened when she saw that Sooze hadn't even opened her bark box. 'You're not trying very hard! Don't you want to dance in the Spring Ceremony?'

'If it happens,' said Sooze glumly.

The branch went silent as everyone stared at each other. What on earth did she mean?

Even Miss Sparkle seemed startled. 'What do you mean? Why wouldn't it happen?'

Sooze bit her lip. 'I mean, um . . . I'll try harder, Miss.'

Miss Sparkle frowned, obviously unconvinced. But before she could say anything else the magpie's call echoed through the school, signalling that the class was over.

'All right, everyone, boxes shut and passed to the

84

front,' said Miss Sparkle. 'And, Sooze – please do try harder tomorrow.'

Twink quickly gathered her things together. Sooze looked so down. *What* was wrong with her? 'I'm just going to have a word with Sooze,' she whispered to Bimi.

Her best friend nodded. 'See if you can get her to talk to you this time!'

As the Daffodil Branch fairies flew out into the trunk, Twink hurried to catch up with Sooze. It wasn't easy – the lavender-haired fairy was skimming away like a meteor!

'Sooze!' called Twink, putting on a burst of speed. 'Wait!'

For a moment she thought Sooze wouldn't stop. Then she did, hovering reluctantly as Twink flew up to her. 'Sooze, what did you mean just now, about the ceremony?'

'Nothing.' Sooze looked away. 'I was just talking rubbish.'

Twink's forehead creased. 'But you sounded so –'

'Oh, just leave me alone!' burst out Sooze.

'Nothing's wrong, all right?'

Twink clenched her fists. 'No, it's not all right!' she snapped. 'You've been moping about for days now. What's *wrong* with you, Sooze? You didn't even act pleased when I finally worked out fairy dust!'

'Who cares if you did!' retorted Sooze. 'Nobody's going to dance in the ceremony anyway –' She stopped short, clasping her hand to her mouth.

Twink's wings went icy-cold. 'What do you mean?'

'I – I just –' Suddenly Sooze burst into tears. 'Oh, flap off!' she cried, covering her face with her hands.

Twink stared at her, shocked. *Sooze*, crying? Sooze never cried! She quickly drew her friend into an empty classroom branch.

'Sooze, please tell me what's wrong,' she begged as they landed on the mossy floor. 'I'm your friend; I want to help.'

'Nobody can help!' sobbed Sooze. 'I'm the only one who can do it, he said so – but I don't know how! I've tried everything, and nothing works –'

'*Sooze!*' Twink gave her friend a gentle shake. 'What are you talking about?'

Sooze gulped and sniffed. Putting her hand in her pocket, she drew out a small object and handed it to Twink. 'This,' she said morosely.

Twink looked down. The object lying in her palm was small and narrow, like two triangles stuck together, and felt cold to the touch. 'But – what is it?'

'A beak,' mumbled Sooze.

Twink blinked in confusion. 'A what?'

'A *beak*,' said Sooze more clearly. She wiped her eyes. 'It – it belongs to the robin on the ice pole.'

Twink's mouth fell open. 'You mean one of the carvings is broken?' she gasped.

Sooze's lips trembled as she nodded. 'I was going to play a prank on Madame, you see, and . . .'

She told Twink everything, finishing with, 'And I've tried *everything* to mend it! I've tried sticking it on with sap glue, and doing a fixing dance, and tying it on with a ribbon – nothing works, nothing, and now the sprites will take the pole away!'

Grabbing the beak back from Twink, Sooze shoved it into her pocket again, her eyes bright with tears.

Twink had listened to Sooze's tale in growing horror.

'But they *can't* take the pole away!' she cried. 'How could they? Then we couldn't turn winter into spring!'

Sooze shrugged miserably. 'I – I suppose not.'

A third-year student flitted past the window, carrying a sparkling ice ornament. 'A bit lower!' she called. 'Yes, that's it – glimmery! Oh, it's looking lovely!'

'But . . .' Twink's throat went dry. Winter not turn into spring? Did that mean the flowers wouldn't bloom? What if it stayed cold and icy for ever?

'Sooze, we have to tell Miss Shimmery,' she whispered.

'No!' Sooze grabbed her arm in a panic. 'Twink, you can't – promise me! Queen Mab will be here any day now – and – and everyone's busy decorating the school, and they'll all know it was my fault!' She looked close to tears again.

Twink shook her head helplessly. 'I know, but what else can we do? You've already tried everything to mend the beak, and –' She stopped as an idea struck her.

'What?' asked Sooze.

'Well, there has to be *some* way to mend it,' said Twink slowly. 'I just wonder if the sprite would give you a hint, if we went back and asked him.'

Sooze's eyes grew wide. 'Oh! Do you think he might?' Then her shoulders sagged again. 'But the sprites aren't speaking to us now. Remember the dance that Madame tried to do – they just ignored her!'

Twink's lavender wings tapped together as she thought. 'Well – maybe Pix will know how we can get them to talk to us,' she said finally. 'Do you mind if we ask her?'

'Not if you think it might help!' Sooze grinned suddenly. 'And – and listen, Opposite, it was pretty glimmery of you to keep on at me. I suppose I did need to tell someone.'

Twink gave her a quick hug. 'That's OK,' she said. 'Don't worry, Sooze, we'll get it sorted! Everything's going to be fine, I'm sure of it.'

Privately, though, Twink wasn't sure at all. Everyone knew how prickly the sprites were. And if Sooze didn't manage to mend the robin . . . what would happen to spring?

Chapter Seven

'All right, let's try this one,' said Pix, squatting beside the frozen pond with a petal book in her hands. 'Ready?'

Twink and Sooze nodded. It was dusk, and a white mist crept over the ground as Pix leaned towards the pond and started to sing.

Sprites down below,
Friends of fairies,
Come say hello,
Please don't tarry!

Twink and Sooze joined in the chorus, fluttering their wings as they sang in lilting harmony. They sang the song over and over again, staring pleadingly at the pond.

Nothing happened.

Their voices faded into silence. Twink swallowed. 'Well –'

'We could try another dance,' said Pix, flipping hurriedly through the pages.

'We've done three already!' burst out Sooze. She stamped her foot. 'Oh! They could at least come out and talk to us!'

'What other dances are there, Pix?' said Twink, squatting down beside her.

Pix paused at a page. 'Well – here's one for helping the algae grow. And there's one to calm down nervous frogs.'

'But nothing else about sprites.' Sooze looked dangerously fed up. Her violet eyes glinted as she tapped her foot on the ground.

'Well – no,' admitted Pix. 'But maybe they'd like it if we helped the algae grow. You know, like a snack, if they're peckish . . .' Her cheeks reddened as Sooze glared at her. 'All right!' Pix burst out. 'We've tried everything and I don't know what else to do. It's hopeless!' She slammed the petal book closed, her yellow wings fluttering in agitation.

Twink's throat tightened. 'Then we don't have a choice. We really *do* have to go to Miss Shimmery.'

'No!' burst out Sooze. 'They're going to come and talk to me – they have to!' She picked up a rock.

'Sooze, no!' Twink grabbed her arm. 'You'll just make them even angrier!'

Sooze shook her off. 'How could I make them *angrier*? Things can't get any worse!'

Pix made a face. 'She's got a point, I suppose.'

'Yes, *thank* you!' Clutching the rock, Sooze flew high above the pond and then dived straight down, whistling through the air like an arrow. As she neared the ice she lifted the rock over her head, ready to fling it. Twink winced, anticipating the crash.

'STOP!' bellowed a watery voice.

Sooze skidded to a startled halt, her legs churning the air as her wings flapped madly. The rock dropped from her grasp, skating harmlessly over the ice.

A sleek green head had popped up through the thin ice at the edge of the pond. 'What destruction is this!' shrieked the sprite. 'First you break our ice pole, now you throw rocks at us!'

Sooze gulped. 'I – I just wanted to talk to you. You see, I –'

'Talk?' screeched the sprite. 'Why should we talk with *you*? You have not mended the pole!'

'But she's been trying,' cried Twink. 'She's done everything she can think of!'

'Pah!' sneered the sprite. 'Glue and dances and ribbons – these things are an insult! There is only one way to fix an ice pole.' Its pale eyes bulged.

'What? What is it?' cried the three girls eagerly.

The sprite bobbed up and down in the water, looking as if it wished it could burst on to the ground and box them about the ears. 'What do you think? Fairy dust, of course! What could be more obvious?'

The tips of Sooze's pointed ears went pale. 'But – I don't know the secret of fairy dust yet,' she faltered.

'Then you cannot mend the pole,' snapped the sprite.

'Couldn't someone *else* mend the pole?' pleaded Twink. 'I could do it, or Pix –'

'No!' said the sprite. It pointed an accusing webbed finger at Sooze. '*That* fairy must mend it. If anyone else tries to, we will take the pole away.'

'But you're probably going to take it away anyway,' pointed out Sooze glumly.

The sprite folded its arms across its scrawny chest. 'Correct! If you have not mended the robin's beak by the time the ceremony starts, we'll sink the ice pole back into the pond and you'll never see it again!'

'But what about turning winter into spring?' cried Twink. 'We have to have the ice pole! You can't just take it away.'

'Hah! Watch us!' And with a splash, the sprite disappeared under the ice again. No amount of cajoling brought it back. Finally the girls looked at each other in dismay.

'Well, I–I guess that's that, then,' said Sooze faintly. 'I've been trying for weeks now to get fairy dust – I don't suppose I'm going to get it in the next day or so.'

'You've got to try!' said Pix. 'You've got over a day, Sooze – there's still time.'

'Think of your family,' said Bimi again. 'That's how *I* got it.'

'I know, you've told me!' Sooze's elbows slumped on the mushroom desk as she glared down at the yellow petal. 'And it still doesn't help. What have *they* got to do with anything?'

Poor Sooze! thought Twink. She looked exhausted. It was almost bedtime, and they had been at it for hours already. Bimi had been let into the secret, and the four of them were all in the empty Fairy Dust branch, having got permission from Miss Sparkle to practise.

A squad of Fourth Years flew past the dark window, checking that all the ice ornaments were in place. The Queen was due to arrive just before dawn. The ceremony was mere hours away – if it took place at all!

The thought chilled Twink down to her pixie boots. 'Come on, Sooze, try just once more!' she urged.

Sooze glanced at her. 'How did you get it?' she asked. 'And *don't* tell me that you thought of your family, or I'll scream!'

Twink hesitated. 'Well – I tried to imagine what Bimi might have done,' she admitted.

Sooze groaned, covering her face with her hands. 'Naturally!'

Twink saw Bimi's mouth tighten as she bit back a reply.

'Just try, Sooze.' Pix rubbed her yellow wing against Sooze's pink one.

Twink held her breath as Sooze reached into her bark box. Closing her eyes, she was silent for a moment – and then she flung the dust in a glittering shower of pink and gold.

The petal stayed the same. The fairies' wings drooped.

'What were you thinking of?' asked Twink in a low voice.

Sooze dropped her chin on her hand. 'I don't know. That – I wanted to get the secret to show my family I could do it. Well, you said to think of my family!' she added defensively as they all looked at each other.

'Not that way, Sooze,' said Bimi tiredly. 'We can't tell you any more, or we'll give it away. But – oh, *can't* you think of something else besides –' She broke off, looking flustered as she realised what she had almost said.

'Besides what?' said Sooze in bewilderment. 'I don't understand!'

'That's just the problem,' muttered Pix. And Twink knew with a sinking heart that she was right. It simply didn't come naturally to Sooze to think of anyone other than herself. It could take her *months* to work out fairy dust!

'Are you girls still in here?' Miss Sparkle hovered in the open doorway, eyebrows raised. 'That's quite enough practice – you must be worn out by now! Time to get ready for bed. I'll put the fairy dust away for you.'

'Oh, please, Miss, just a few more minutes!' burst out Sooze. 'I really want to dance in the ceremony –'

Miss Sparkle shook her head gently. 'I'm sorry that you haven't got it yet, Sooze, but never mind; watching the Spring Ceremony will be lovely as well. Now come on, flitter-flutter.'

Despair swept over Twink as she and the others flew slowly from the room. Sooze would never have a chance to get it now. What on earth were they going to do?

'No,' said Sooze.

'But, Sooze, we have to!' whispered Twink. They were in the bath-branch, rubbing their arms with soft mossy sponges. Walnut buckets of fresh water stood on mushroom stands.

'*No*,' repeated Sooze. 'I am absolutely not going to tell Miss Shimmery. And you can't, either – promise me, all of you!' She glanced at Pix and Bimi, who were washing nearby.

'But, Sooze, it's not being a tell-tale, don't you see?' said Bimi miserably. 'What if the sprites really take the ice pole away? There won't be any spring!'

'And the *Queen's* going to be here,' added Pix. 'We can't just keep quiet about it.'

Bright tears shone in Sooze's eyes as she scrubbed at her arms. 'Maybe I'll still get the secret in time.'

'Oh, Sooze . . .' Twink trailed off.

'I *might*.' Sooze wiped her eyes. 'Maybe I just need to really feel under pressure. I'll get some fairy dust off Winn before breakfast. I bet I'll work it out once the Queen gets here.'

'But we can't wait until then!' cried Twink. 'Everyone will be down at the pond, ready for the ceremony to start!'

'And besides, then you'd have to mend the pole in front of the whole school,' pointed out Bimi. She looked horrified at the thought.

Sooze flung her sponge back into the bucket with a splash. 'Well, that's better than telling everyone that I broke it and there's not going to be a spring this year!'

'I don't know, Sooze . . .' Pix tapped her wings together. 'I think we should fly up to Miss Shimmery's office and tell her the truth.'

'*No!*' Sooze glanced quickly around and lowered her voice again, her fists clenched. 'It's not your secret to tell. If I don't get it before the ceremony starts, I'll tell then, I promise. But just give me a little bit more time!'

Chapter
Eight

Stars still shone in the sky as the school gathered at the pond, waiting for Queen Mab and her retinue to arrive. The ice ornaments that hung on the branches of Glitterwings moved gently in the wind, twinkling like hundreds of captured diamonds.

The ice pole rose from the centre of the pond, as mysterious and beautiful as ever. From where Twink hovered with the rest of the first year, she could just see the jagged edge of the robin's broken beak. She shivered, remembering how furious the sprite had been.

Sooze looked pale and frightened. She, too, was staring at the broken beak – and from the expression on her face, Twink knew that she hadn't worked out the secret to fairy dust yet.

A shiver of dread ran through Twink. Miss Shimmery and the other teachers all looked so serious, so solemn. The students all had tiny pouches of fairy dust at their hips, and were dressed in their prettiest flower dresses, hushed and expectant as they waited for the Queen.

And it was all going to go horribly, horribly wrong.

Bimi nudged her. 'This is awful!' she whispered. 'We can't just hover here and not say anything, can we?'

'We promised,' Twink reluctantly whispered back. 'I suppose we should give her a bit more time.'

'But the Queen will be here any –'

Bimi broke off as a pair of stately silver butterflies appeared over the hill. They circled low over the assembled fairies, dipping their wings.

'The Queen's coming!' cried someone.

Twink's breath caught despite her worries. As one, the school drifted to the ground and rose up on their tiptoes, bowing their heads respectfully. Twink couldn't help herself. She peeked out from under her pink hair, craning to see.

A flock of the most beautiful fairies she had ever seen was approaching. Queen Mab's counsellors were dressed in the most gorgeous, exotic flowers imaginable, in every colour of the rainbow. They sang a song of welcome as they came, their voices like shimmering silver chimes.

And then – there was Queen Mab! Twink gasped. The beloved fairy queen was centuries old, but her face still glowed with beauty. Her blonde hair waved gently about her face as she flew, and her golden wings gleamed in the pale starlight.

The Queen and her retinue landed on the icy lawn.

Miss Shimmery flitted forward, holding out both hands. 'Welcome to Glitterwings Academy, Your Majesty. We are honoured to have you.'

The two fairy women kissed each other's cheeks.

Queen Mab's white lily dress sparkled with seed pearls. A matching seed-pearl coronet rested on her shining blonde hair.

Oh, Sooze, please work out the secret! thought Twink fervently. The lavender-haired fairy had her eyes closed, and looked like she was concentrating hard.

Miss Shimmery escorted Queen Mab to the mushroom grandstand that Miss Petal and the older students had grown for her the day before. The mushrooms shone pure silver in the faint light,

festooned with icy ribbons and bows.

Queen Mab turned to face the students. 'Doesn't Glitterwings look beautiful!' she exclaimed. Her voice was so low and lovely that thrills crept across Twink's arms. 'Thank you, girls. I know that you will do a wonderful job of seeing in the spring.'

She sat on the highest mushroom, her golden wings fluttering. Her counsellors took their places around her.

Miss Shimmery bowed her head with a smile. 'I think we're almost ready to begin.'

Sooze! thought Twink. *Don't just stand there,* SAY *something!*

But Sooze didn't speak. Twink, Bimi and Pix shared an agonised look as Miss Shimmery flew back to the students and hovered in front of them. 'Dancers, take your positions. Those students who are not taking part, please sit quietly on the ground.'

With a solemn rustle, the school spread its wings and started to fly forward. Twink didn't move. She felt as if her wings had frozen together. Oh, *wasn't* Sooze going to say anything?

If Sooze wouldn't, then she would have to. Twink licked dry lips, and opened her mouth to speak.

'Wait!' burst out Sooze suddenly. 'WAIT! We can't begin the dance yet.'

Twink slumped in relief as Sooze skimmed quickly over to Miss Shimmery. The school hovered over the pond in surprise, watching as Sooze seemed to explain something, red-faced. Finally she reached her hand in her pocket and pulled out an object, which she showed to Miss Shimmery.

The HeadFairy's expression was grave. She said something to Sooze. Sooze shook her head, and looked close to tears.

Twink clutched Bimi's hand. Neither fairy could speak. Oh, *what* was being said?

Finally Miss Shimmery turned to the school, her rainbow wings gleaming as they opened and closed. 'There is a problem,' she announced. 'The ice pole has been broken, and it must be mended by Sooze Birdsong, otherwise the dance cannot go ahead.'

There was a stunned silence. Up on the grandstand, the Queen's counsellors leaned together, whispering. Queen Mab herself sat very still and straight, watching the proceedings keenly.

'But I *can't* mend it,' cried Sooze. 'I don't know how to use fairy dust!'

'You must try again now,' said Miss Shimmery gently. 'We cannot do it for you, Sooze. I've no doubt that the sprites meant exactly what they said.'

The school hovered silently in place – hundreds of brightly dressed fairies, all of them watching Sooze with anxious eyes. On the horizon, the stars were beginning to fade.

'Quickly, Sooze!' said Miss Shimmery. 'It will be dawn soon.'

Sooze hovered wretchedly, biting her lip. Watching her, Twink knew that she had no more idea than before how to use fairy dust.

Suddenly Twink couldn't bear it any more. Dropping Bimi's hand, she darted into the air and flew to Sooze's side. Surprised murmurs rippled through the crowd.

'Oh, Opposite, what am I going to do?' whispered Sooze, clutching her hand. 'I can't mend it!'

'You *can*,' said Twink firmly. 'Sooze, look at everyone. Think about how hard they've all worked.'

'I don't –' started Sooze.

'Look at Glitterwings!' broke in Twink desperately. 'Each of those ice ornaments had to be made separately, and then hung by one of the students. Hundreds of them! Think about how much time that took.'

Sooze turned and looked at the school, a frown creasing her forehead.

'Think about Glitterwings,' whispered Twink. 'You love it, Sooze, I know you do. Think about how everyone would feel if the ceremony didn't go ahead.'

Twink started to say more, and then stopped, holding her breath. Sooze's frown had cleared. Her violet eyes grew wide as she stared at Glitterwings, and then at the silent, hovering students.

'I – I think I understand,' said Sooze in wonder. 'Oh, Twink, I think I get it!'

Before Twink could answer, Sooze had jetted off,

her pink wings fluttering as fast as they could. Flying straight to the ice pole, Sooze hovered near its top. Pressing the icy beak against the robin's face, she closed her eyes and reached into her other pocket.

As the school watched in hopeful silence, Sooze concentrated for a moment, clenching a pinch of dust. Then she flung it at the beak.

A burst of pink and gold light lit the top of the pole. The beak was part of the robin once again, shining like new.

'I did it!' cried Sooze jubilantly. 'Oh, I really did it!'

'Well done!' said Miss Shimmery warmly. 'Now to your places, girls – quickly! Dawn will be breaking at any moment.'

The school flew hurriedly into place. Twink joined the others, taking hold of one of the icy strands. As Madame Brightfoot had explained, this was not a dance that needed to be learned. The ice pole itself would lead them; all they had to do was follow.

Sure enough, Twink felt a faint pressure against her hand as her strand twitched into life. The ice pole began to slowly rotate, plaiting its strands into an intricate pattern.

Oh! Twink felt a rush of pleasure as the strands wove about. Suddenly she felt like doing somersaults, like twirling and tumbling! She couldn't resist. No one could. They spun and dipped and frolicked, whooping with joy. Below, Twink could just see the water sprites through the ice, dancing along with them.

Laughter bubbled up in Twink's throat. Bringing in the spring wasn't solemn at all. It was the most glimmery fun in the world!

Finally the strands slowed and stopped. It was time.

Reaching into her pouch, Twink closed her eyes. *For springtime*, she thought. *For all the creatures and plants and flowers in the world!* And as she flung the dust at her strand, she thought, *Goodbye, winter. We'll see you again next year!*

As all the fairies did the same, pink and gold light

burst over the ice pole. It shimmered like liquid fire. Twink held her breath.

Slowly, so slowly that she almost didn't notice at first, her strand began to turn green. First one small, curling tendril appeared, and then another. All at once, green flowed up the strand as it became a vine of ivy. Bright flowers appeared, weaving around the ivy's heart-shaped leaves.

The other strands were bursting into life as well. Twink caught Sooze's eye, and the two fairies grinned at each other. Sooze looked happier than Twink had ever seen her – not mischievous, or eagerly plotting a prank, but just *happy*.

The ice pole melted away into warm, living colours as the carved creatures came to life. A badger sat up, blinking its eyes and twitching its black nose. Several field mice scampered down the pole and ran across the ice, squeaking joyfully.

Just as the first ray of spring sunshine shone on to the pole, the robin at its top opened its beak and began to sing.

'The ice pole is now a green pole,' announced

Miss Shimmery. Her smile was as warm as the new sunshine. 'Thank you, girls. Welcome to the spring!'

There was a party afterwards, with the fairies all mingling on the lawn, sipping fizzy dew and eating honey cake. Already, the morning felt warmer than before, with new leaves and flowers bursting up everywhere they looked. Twink and her friends sat in the sunshine beside the pond. The ice had already melted, but the pole remained, covered in bright flowers.

'Isn't it glimmery!' sighed Bimi, leaning back

against a dandelion. 'Oh, Sooze, I'm so glad you got the secret!'

'It was down to Twink, really,' said Sooze shyly. 'I never would have got it on my own.' She glanced at Twink. 'Thanks, Opposite.'

Before Twink could answer, a familiar green head popped up through the water. 'And just in time!' snapped the sprite. 'We thought we'd have to take the pole away after all.'

'You wouldn't have really done it, would you?' asked Twink. 'I mean, not *really*?'

The sprite stared haughtily at her. 'We always keep our word, even where silly young fairies are concerned. Goodbye, young fairy – I hope we don't meet again!' And with that, the sprite bowed solemnly to Sooze, and flipped back into the pond.

The friends looked at each other, and suddenly burst into laughter. 'That's you told, Sooze,' giggled Bimi.

'Oh, flap off!' Sooze's cheeks were red as she grinned. 'Anyway, I suppose I can't blame it.'

Twink laughed with the others, but her smile

became wistful as she glanced across at Queen Mab and her retinue, preparing to leave. Athough the Queen had mingled with the students after the ceremony, Twink had been far too shy to approach her.

She sighed, and sipped her fizzy dew glumly. She'd probably never have another chance, now. Why should an ordinary fairy like her meet the Queen?

'Hello, girls,' said a voice.

The fairies jumped to their feet as Miss Shimmery landed beside them. 'Well done, Sooze,' said the HeadFairy. 'I knew you could do it!'

'Thank you, Miss Shimmery,' said Sooze in a small voice. 'Er – am I going to be punished?'

Miss Shimmery laughed. 'Well, I think you know now that playing pranks near the ice pole wasn't the wisest idea in the world! I daresay you've been punished enough already – you must have gone through quite a worrying time.'

'Oh, yes, Miss Shimmery,' nodded Sooze fervently. 'I really have. It's been awful!'

Miss Shimmery's rainbow wings gleamed in the sunshine. 'And just to make sure you don't forget the lesson, I think I'll put you in charge of tending the green pole once the new term begins. You'll need to transplant all the ivy and flowers somewhere else, where they can really thrive.'

Twink knew that Sooze would once have moaned at the prospect of so much hard work. Now she fluttered her wings eagerly, eyes shining. 'Yes, Miss Shimmery. I'd really like to!'

'Good,' smiled Miss Shimmery. 'Now then, Twink – Queen Mab would like a word with you before she flies off.'

Twink started, and dropped her acorn cup. Her friends gaped at her. '*Me?*' she gasped.

'Yes, you.' Miss Shimmery lifted off the ground and hovered, motioning to Twink. 'Come along, my dear – she has to leave soon.'

In a daze, Twink flew along beside Miss Shimmery. As they approached Queen Mab and her retinue, she saw Mariella and Lola sidle up next to the Queen. They tiptoed respectfully, and Mariella said something.

As Twink landed, she heard Queen Mab reply,

'Why, of course I remember your grandmother!'

Mariella tossed her hair and smirked at Lola. 'See, I told you,' she mouthed. Lola looked on, wide-eyed with awe.

'She was one of the best cleaning fairies I've ever had,' continued the Queen.

Mariella looked like she had swallowed a hot chilli seed. 'A – a *cleaning* fairy?' she spluttered.

Queen Mab nodded. 'Yes, that's right. A charming fairy; we were great friends. There is nothing wrong with being a cleaning fairy, my girl. You had better not be so snobbish, or you won't find many friends.'

A smile lit her lovely face as she caught sight of Twink. 'Ah! Twink Flutterby. I've heard so much about you.' The Queen clasped Twink's hand as Twink gave a hasty tiptoe.

'Me?' whispered Twink. 'But all I did was to have a word with Sooze. She's the one who got the secret.' Out of the corner of her eye, she saw Mariella flounce off with a scowl.

The Queen's eyes were bright blue, and seemed to

look right into Twink's very soul. Twink trembled, wondering what she was going to say.

Queen Mab smiled. 'I must go now, Twink, but we'll meet again, I'm sure of it. And I shall look forward to it very much. You're a very special young fairy, my dear.' Stooping, she kissed Twink lightly on both cheeks.

'Thank you, Your Majesty,' murmured Twink in a dream.

She stood in silent wonder as the Queen bid farewell to Miss Shimmery, and then lifted off into the air with her counsellors. The seed pearls on the Queen's lily dress sparkled in the sunlight as they flew away, the silver butterflies following close behind.

Miss Shimmery rested a hand on her shoulder. 'Well done, my dear.'

'But – but I don't understand,' said Twink in bewilderment. 'Why did she want to meet *me*?'

The HeadFairy smiled gently at her. 'You haven't worked it out, then? The reason why Queen Mab decided that Glitterwings should host the Spring

Ceremony?'

Twink shook her head mutely.

'It was because of you, Twink,' said Miss Shimmery. 'Because of how you helped Stripe last term. The Queen wanted to meet the fairy who made friends with a wasp – and it inspired her to mend the bridges between the fairies and the water sprites, as well.' She laughed suddenly. 'Of course, *that* almost didn't go as planned because of Sooze's prank . . . but we got there in the end!'

Twink's thoughts spun as she watched the Queen and her retinue disappear from view. Queen Mab had wanted to meet *her*. Her – Twink Flutterby! It was too incredible to be true.

Yet it had happened. It really had.

'My father was right,' said Twink. 'This is one term I'll never, ever forget!'

'Me neither,' said Bimi. The two friends smiled at each other.

The Daffodil Branch fairies were busy packing their things, getting ready to go home for the spring

holiday. Sooze grinned as she tied her oak-leaf bag shut. 'And the best thing is we'll be Second Years next term! We'll be able to use fairy dust all we like! Oh – just *think* of the pranks we can play –'

'*Sooze!*' cried the rest of the Branch.

'You're not thinking of playing more pranks!' gasped Twink, half-laughing.

Sooze tossed her hair back. 'Well, why not?' she said with a cheeky smile. 'You can't be good *all* the time. I'll just take care that there aren't any ice poles around!'

Twink laughed. Sooze would never change, not really – and deep down, Twink was glad of it.

'Well, I don't think it's fair at all,' snapped Mariella. 'And you even got to dance in the ceremony, when *I* didn't! Why, you should have been expelled! When I tell my mother what happened, I bet –'

'Oh, *please* do!' broke in Sooze. 'Maybe she'll finally send you somewhere else. If we all wrote to her and begged, d'you think she might?' She clasped her hands under her chin pleadingly.

Mariella glared and flounced away as the branch erupted into laughter. Twink grinned to herself. Mariella would never change either, that was clear!

Finally the packing was done. After a flurry of goodbye hugs and cries of 'See you next term!' Twink picked up her bag and flitted to the doorway. Her parents were probably waiting outside by now, eager to hear all about the ceremony. She could hardly wait to tell them everything – but even so, she paused and looked back at comfortable, cosy Daffodil Branch, where she had spent so many hours and had grown so much.

They'd be in a new branch next term. Second-year fairies – not the babies of the school any more.

'Goodbye, Daffodil Branch,' whispered Twink softly. 'And – thanks a lot!'

The End

From Fledge Star

A new year at Glitterwings! Twink Flutterby flew eagerly over the flower-covered hill. Almost there . . . almost . . . and then, there it was! The great oak tree that housed Glitterwings Academy came into view, its leaves bursting with springtime. The tiny windows that wound their way up its trunk shone like pieces of sunshine.

'Isn't it beautiful!' exclaimed Twink's grandmother, flying beside her. She was accompanying Twink to school this term, as Twink's parents were at a Fairy Medics' convention. 'I can see why you love it so much, my dear.'

Twink nodded happily. 'It's the most wonderful school in the world.'

Down below, a first-year student rode on a mouse, with her parents flying along overhead. The young fairy glanced up at Twink admiringly, and Twink felt very grown-up all of a sudden. She and her friends were Second Years now – not the babies of the school any longer.

Titania Woods

There are lots more stories about Glitterwings
Academy – make sure you haven't missed any of them!

If you have any difficulty in finding these in your local bookshop,
please visit www.bloomsbury.com or call 020 7440 2475
to order direct from Bloomsbury Publishing.

Visit www.glitterwingsacademy.co.uk for more fabulous fairy fun!